TIGER MOTH

THE DUNG BEETLE
BANDITS

Librarian Reviewer
Allyson A. W. Lyga, MS
Library Media/Graphic Novel Consultant
Fulbright Memorial Fund Scholar, author

Reading Consultant
Elizabeth Stedem
Educator/Consultant, Colorado Springs, CO
MA in Elementary Education, University of Denver, CO

STONE ARCH BOOKS
MINNEAPOLIS   SAN DIEGO

Graphic Sparks are published by Stone Arch Books,
151 Good Counsel Drive, P.O. Box 669,
Mankato, Minnesota 56002.
www.stonearchbooks.com

Library of Congress Cataloging-in-Publication Data
Reynolds, Aaron, 1970–
    The Dung Beetle Bandits / by Aaron Reynolds; illustrated by Erik Lervold.
    p. cm. — (Graphic Sparks. Tiger Moth)
    ISBN-13: 978-1-59889-317-5 (library binding)
    ISBN-10: 1-59889-317-3 (library binding)
    ISBN-13: 978-1-59889-412-7 (paperback)
    ISBN-10: 1-59889-412-9 (paperback)
    1. Graphic novels. I. Lervold, Erik. II. Title.
PN6727.R45D86 2007
741.5'973—dc22   2006028028

Summary: Tiger Moth and his sidekick, Kung Pow, visit a dung beetle ranch owned by
Tiger's Uncle Aphid. Thundering tarnation! The beetles are missing! It looks like the work
of that varmint rustler Stinky McCree. Tiger is convinced, however, that somewhere out
among the desert cacti, a darker evil lurks. And what's that gross stuff on Kung's hand?

Art Director: Heather Kindseth
Graphic Designer: Brann Garvey

1 2 3 4 5 6 12 11 10 09 08 07

Printed in the United States of America

TIGER MOTH

THE DUNG BEETLE
BANDITS

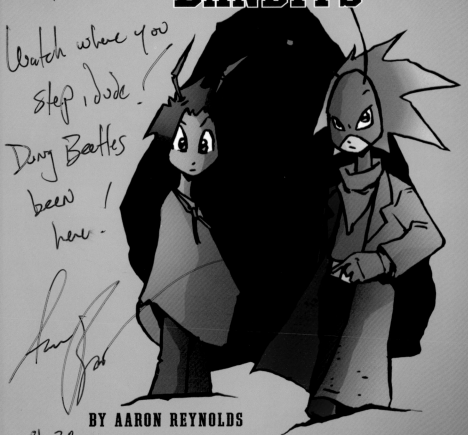

To Kevin,

Watch where you
step, dude!
Dung Beetles
been
here.

01-28-07

BY AARON REYNOLDS

ILLUSTRATED BY ERIC LERVOLD

Cast of Characters

Mrs. Mandible

Tiger Moth

Kung Pow

Uncle Aphid

Stinky McKree

Ahhh. There's nothing quite like the smell of a school bus when you'd normally be doing times tables.

I can't believe your uncle actually owns a beetle ranch.

Is it so hard for you to believe that there's *cowboy* blood running through my veins?

Actually, yes.

Yeah, I know

Uncle Aphid had invited my class out to his ranch for a field trip. Beetle ranch, bug spray factory, it didn't make much difference to me. A field trip is a field trip.

But when we arrived . . .

Mr. Aphid, thank you so much for inviting my class.

Sure thing there, Miss Mandible, I'm right glad to have you.

I just wish it was under better conditions, is all.

Whatever is the problem, Mr. Aphid?

Yeah, Uncle Aphid, what's going on?

My ninja nose sniffed trouble in the wind.

My ninja nose was working overtime.

What is that smell?

Uncle, you didn't eat chili for breakfast, did you?

Not today.

That's nasty, Kung Pow! Give a little warning before you whip one off like that.

Don't look at me! Whoever smelt it, dealt it!

Well, if it's not any of us . . .

Hold on! I just caught me a whiff of it too!

That smell is stinkbug!

14

Uncle Aphid sweet-talked Mrs. Mandible into letting us help him. If you ask me, she was fluttering her eyelashes at him just enough to unsettle my stomach. Ewwww!

An hour later we were riding Uncle Aphid's fastest horseflies and making a beeline for the horizon.

Ow! Ow!

This pillbug was not designed for saddle-sitting.

What's wrong, Kung Pow? Ants in your pants?

Hang tough, Kung. We've got to be close. 120 dung beetles can't just disappear into thin air.

Suddenly, the trail disappeared into thin air.

Thundering tarnation! End of the trail.

Now what, Mr. Aphid?

The creek's not too far from here. You boys stay here. I'll go see if there's anything worth seeing down there.

Good. My saddle sores could use the rest.

Something doesn't add up here.

Pew, Kung Pow!
On second
thought, maybe
lay off the jerky.

20

I didn't do anything!

Well, if you didn't do it, then something smells really bad in prickly-ville.

For the third time that day, my super-sonic ninja nose kicked in.

Bingo!

21

You want some nose plugs before you go in there?

Not on your life. I'm following my nose on this one.

Great. A tunnel filled with 120 dung beetles and a stinkbug. Sounds like a party for the nostrils.

The tunnel creeped and crawled its way deeper underground, but long before I smelled anything more . . .

Listen!

It is!

It's the crime bug king of the underworld . . .

Weevil!

SLAM!

RUMBLE RUMBLE RUMBLE RUMBLE RUMBLE

Oooh! Squished like a bug.

But Stinky McKree and his dung beetle bandits were put in their place.

The cases of tainted meat were found in the cave, and disposed of. The town was saved from a nasty outbreak of mad bug disease.

Uncle Aphid's dung beetles were returned to their rightful owner.

All thanks to the quick wits and keen nose of Tiger Moth: Insect Ninja.

There was only one thing left that was smelling rotten.

ABOUT THE AUTHOR

Aaron Reynolds loves bugs and loves books, so Tiger Moth was a perfect blend of both. Aaron is the author of several great books for kids, including *Chicks and Salsa*, which *Publishers Weekly* called "a literary fandango" that "even confirmed macaroni-and-cheese lovers will devour." Aaron had no idea what a "fandango" was, but after looking it up in the dictionary (it means "playful and silly behavior"), he hopes to write several more fandangos in the future. He lives near Chicago with his wife, two kids, and four insect-obsessed cats.

ABOUT THE ILLUSTRATOR

Erik Lervold was born in Puerto Rico, a small island in the Caribbean, and has been a professional painter. He attended college at the University of Puerto Rico's Mayaguez campus, where he majored in Civil Engineering. Deciding that he wanted to be a full-time artist, he moved to Florida, New York, Chicago, Duluth, and finally Minneapolis. He attended the Minneapolis College of Art and Design, majored in Comic Art, and graduated in 2004. Erik teaches classes in libraries in the Minneapolis area, and has taught art in the Minnesota Children's Museum. He loves the *color green* and has a bunch of really big goggles. He also loves sandwiches. If you want him to be your friend, bring him a roast beef sandwich and he will love you forever.

GLOSSARY

aphid (AY-fid)-a bug that that sucks juice out of plants, like a cactus or a yucca plant

bronco (BRONG-ko)-a cowboy name for a horse that lives out on the desert

corral (kor-AL)-a fenced area to keep horses or cattle or dung beetles

cringe (KRINJ)-to shrink away from something in fear. People who don't like beetles or aphids, might cringe when they see them.

rustle (RUS-uhl)-to steal horses or cattle (or dung beetles)

scallywag (SKAL-ee-wag)-cowboy talk for a **varmint**. See below.

taint (TAYNT)-to make something yucky or sick

vamoosed (va-MOOST)-cowboy talk for gone, vanished, or run away

varmint (VAR-mint)-cowboy talk for a criminal or bad person

whippersnapper (WIP-ur-snap-ur)-a grownup word for a kid who's noisy or energetic; a brat or a super hero.

FROM THE NINJA NOTEBOOK

Dung Beetles and Other Desert Bugs

Dung beetles get their name from their habit of feeding on dung, or animal waste products.

Some dung beetles called rollers, use their back legs to roll dung into a smooth, tiny ball.

Ranchers like dung beetles. The little critters move the dung away from the cattle who made it. Since dung can attract flies and other bugs, the dung beetles keep the cattle free from pests.

The ancient Egyptians believed that the sun was rolled across the sky by a gigantic dung beetle named Khepri.

The deadliest bug in the U.S. desert is the Black Widow spider. A female Black Widow is 15 times more poisonous than a rattlesnake!

Desert tarantulas are hairy spiders that grow up to 3 inches long and live in the Southwestern United States. They are non-poisonous and make great house pets!

Yucca moths are very helpful to the yucca plants. Without the tiny fliers, the prickly yuccas would not get pollinated.

Darkling beetles have a *cool* way of getting water in the dry desert. Drops of early morning fog turn into liquid on their smooth, shiny front wings.

DISCUSSION QUESTIONS

1. Have you ever been on a field trip to a farm or a ranch? Would you like to go on one? Why or why not?

2. Uncle Aphid seems like a cool uncle. Do you have any relatives that have unusual jobs or live in unusual places?

3. Tiger Moth and Kung Pow are both eager to help Uncle Aphid find his dung beetles. But Kung Pow isn't very excited about being out in the country. Why don't you think he likes cowboy life as much as Tiger Moth seems to?

WRITING PROMPTS

1. Imagine you can ride a horsefly just like Tiger Moth and Kung Pow. Where would you fly? What does it feel like? Is the buzzing of the wings too loud for you to hear other sounds? Write a description of your amazing flight.

2. Kung Pow does not like getting stinkbug goo on his hand. He wants to wash it off right away. Have you ever gotten real dirty working on a chore? Write what the chore was and how you had to clean up.

3. Uncle Aphid is very upset when he finds his dung beetles have been rustled. Have you ever lost something that meant a lot to you? Do you know someone who had something stolen? Write and tell what happened.

INTERNET SITES

Do you want to know more about subjects related to this book? Or are you interested in learning about other topics? Then check out FactHound, a fun, easy way to find Internet sites.

Our investigative staff has already sniffed out great sites for you!

Here's how to use FactHound:

1. Visit www.facthound.com

2. Select your grade level.

3. To learn more about subjects related to this book, type in the book's ISBN number: **1598893173.**

4. Click the **Fetch It** button.

FactHound will fetch the best Internet sites for you!